The Square Root of Falling

A BRAZOS HIGH ROMANCE

AMY SPARLING

ONE

JULES

When my alarm goes off at 6:40 in the morning, I've already been awake for an hour. It's not like I planned it or wanted this early bird morning. It was just really, really hard to sleep last night knowing that today is the first day of my junior year of high school. I remember the young, innocent, (and frankly stupid) me back in my freshman year. I was so excited to get to high school that I jumped out of bed and eagerly got dressed in the outfit I'd picked out weeks before after a day spent at the mall shopping for the perfect first day attire. Oh, that poor innocent version of me. That Jules Minuti had no idea what would happen to her just two years later.

I throw my blankets off and sit up in bed, letting out a frustrated groan. I didn't pick out my outfit last night. In fact, I didn't even go shopping for new school clothes this year because I just didn't care. New school clothes imply that you want to look nice. Looking nice means you want other people to think you look nice.

And the only reason I've ever wanted to look nice was so that boys would like me. That is not who I am anymore.

I snort sarcastically as I shuffle toward my closet and fling open the door. I do not want boys to like me this year. In fact, I am *so* over boys this year. Maybe even forever.

I grab the first Brazos High T-shirt I find and then retrieve a pair of jeans off my closet floor. I wore them a few days ago but they don't look dirty. Eh, good enough.

I get dressed and pull my hair into a ponytail and then stare at my reflection in the bathroom mirror as I brush my teeth. All my makeup sits neatly in the makeup caddy next to my sink, but it's just going to stay there. I cannot be bothered to get all dolled up for the stupid first day of school.

My carefree, no-nonsense attitude lasts for exactly five minutes, give or take. Then suddenly I'm breaking down. It happens when I'm walking out to the kitchen where my mom is drinking coffee and waiting on her toast and my dad is watching the news in the living room because he works from home and doesn't really get started working until noon most days.

It's right about here, when I grab a blueberry muffin from the pantry, that I feel my chest break open.

Not literally, of course.

It's a metaphorical break, but the pain is real.

I told myself this wouldn't happen. I spent all summer telling myself I'd be okay. That I'd move on and go to school and be fine. I dig my teeth into my bottom lip as I pour a cup of orange juice and take a bite of my muffin.

I guess all those words I told myself were just lies because it still hurts and I am still not over it.

Not over *him*.

I grit my teeth, draw in a deep breath, and take another huge bite of my muffin. You can't possibly cry while eating a blueberry muffin, right? It would go against the laws of physics or baking or something.

Mom spreads strawberry jam on her toast and then sits next to me at the kitchen table. "You ready for the first day of school?" she asks.

I shrug. "I suppose."

"Only two more years left and you'll be all grown up."

I shrug again. *I will not cry.*

I will not think about *him.*

The only good thing about my life right now is that I finally turned sixteen last May and now I can drive myself to school. I have one of those weird late birthdays where everyone else in my sophomore class turned sixteen way earlier than I did. But I'm finally the legal age to drive, and my mom did the most amazing thing and gave me her car over the summer. She got a new car for herself, and I got to be the lucky recipient of a slightly old, slightly scratched up, but totally amazing Chevrolet Cruise. It's mine, all mine, and I finally get to drive myself to school. Woohoo!

My excitement wanes as I make the short drive across town to my school. It doesn't matter how much I try to distract myself, or how much I lie and tell my heart it doesn't need to hurt anymore, I'm still hurt. It's been three and a half months and yet... still hurt.

I hate this.

I hate him.

Trevor Blankenship was my first "real" boyfriend. He asked me out to the homecoming dance in August of my sophomore year and we were inseparable ever since. He was tall and cute and he really liked me. He'd write me love letters on actual paper instead of through text. But he sent me love letters through text too. We met up before every class and held hands while we walked to our next class. He'd wait for me after school and drive me home. I was totally smitten. My mom says that teenagers don't really know what love is, and I guess I understand where she's coming from, because we don't have years of life experience or whatever. That's why I won't say that I *loved* him... what I felt for him was definitely real and strong and over-whelming. If it wasn't real love, it was something very close to it.

I thought we would be together forever. I had daydreams of the vows I'd recite at our wedding, talking about how he was my high school sweetheart and my first real boyfriend and how now he'd be my forever soul mate. What a fool I was.

It was just one week before my birthday, back in May. It was a Sunday. The night before, Trevor had gone to a house party with some of our friends, but I wasn't able to go because my mom didn't want me out that late. My curfew was 10:00p.m. until I turned 16. But Trevor went to the party without me, and I guess whatever happened there made him decide to break my heart.

Sunday morning, I'd woken up, texted him hello with what I now feel is an embarrassing number of heart emojis (ugh), and then I wondered why I didn't get a reply back. Two whole hours went by, which was by far the longest we'd ever been without texting. Finally, I checked Snapchat and that's when the worst day of my life unfolded.

Trevor had posted a bunch of Snaps to his story. I will not relive them all right now because I really don't want to cry, but suffice it to say he posted stuff saying he decided to be single now.

My boyfriend broke up with me on Snapchat.

I swallow down the ball of anger that rises in my throat. I must have relived those awful memories a little too deeply just now because now I'm arriving at school and I don't even remember driving here. I turn into the student parking lot and find a spot to park. This is my first time driving to school, and I choose a parking spot way in the back. I don't know why. It just feels right. Parking back here away from everyone is kind of a metaphor for how I'm going to live out my junior year. Not *alone* exactly, but single.

I'm not totally alone. I have Abby, who is the greatest friend in the world, and several other friends. Platonic friends. I made this choice a few weeks ago while I was crying over a pint of mint chocolate chip ice cream, and I am not backing down on it.

This school year will be all about my studies. Not boys.

I won't date. I won't flirt. I won't so much as look at a cute boy this year. Why? Because it's just not worth it. Boys are stupid. Dating is stupid.

High school sweethearts are stupid.

After suffering through weeks of heartache and nights of crying myself to sleep, I now have a brand new philosophy in life:

You can't get a broken heart if you don't date anyone.

I park my car and hang up my new Brazos High parking pass over my rearview mirror. My hands grip the steering wheel as I stare ahead at my school, a two-story building that's been here forever. My parents went to Brazos High School. I wonder how many hearts have been broken at this place. Probably way too many. But that's on them because those people were dumb enough to fall in love and get their hearts broken. I won't make that mistake twice. Nope.

The first day of school means we all meet in the

cafeteria to get our class schedules. I head to the table marked M-R since my last name is Minuti, and I wait in line to get my schedule. Coach Branson hands it to me and when I turn around, I smack straight into my best friend.

"Please tell me we have classes together," Abby says, handing me her schedule. Abby is short with long dark hair and tanned skin. We've been best friends forever, because unlike boyfriends, Abby won't break up with me over Snapchat.

I hold our class schedules next to each other and skim down the list. I have math first, which is kind of good because it's a hard class and I'm more functional first thing in the morning. Abby has cosmetology first period. But we have History together for second, and we have the same lunch, and then Interpersonal Studies together in seventh period. That one was a given because not many people take that elective class. We signed up for it together hoping we'd get in the same class, and we did.

"Two classes and lunch," I say, handing it back to her.

She frowns. "Blah. Better than no classes, I guess." She puts a hand on my shoulder. "How are you doing?"

"I'm doing perfectly fine," I say with a haughty

tone that makes her laugh. I keep up the tone and put on a snooty accent. "Why on earth would you even ask such a thing?"

She rolls her eyes. "You know why I'm asking. You might run into you-know-who today... I'm just looking out for you."

I make a gagging sound. "I am so over you-know-you. I don't care if I see him. I don't care to see any boys, actually."

She looks like she doesn't believe me, but she doesn't say anything. I hook my arm through her elbow. "Let's go get some coffee."

Last year, the school decided to raise money by selling coffee from little coffee carts in the cafeteria. It was a huge success, and the students love it. I didn't much care for coffee until these coffee carts arrived on campus, and now I love a hot cup of dark roast with hazelnut creamer. It's my morning ritual.

We get our coffees and start walking toward the main hallway. Abby grabs my arm. "Don't look to your left," she whispers. "Evil ex-boyfriend alert."

I scoff like it's no big deal, but inside, my heart is pounding. "I really don't care," I say, looking straight ahead. "I am so over him."

"I'm just looking out for you," Abby says. She saw me cry so many times over the summer that it's no wonder she doesn't believe that I'm totally over Trevor.

But maybe I don't believe it, either. Because the only thing I want to do is look to my left to see if I can spot him.

Luckily, I'm strong enough to resist.

TWO

JAKE

Sweat drips down my forehead and I don't even bother to wipe it off. There's no point because the back of my hand is also coated in sweat and the air is thick with early morning humidity that clings to my clothes and every inch of my body. My feet trudge on, my shoes soaked from the dewy grass as I make my fifth lap around the high school. The rest of the soccer team is here, too. We are all being punished for something I did not do.

This past weekend, a few Varsity players decided to have a party out at the lake. Not only was the alcohol abundant, the incriminating photos they took of themselves and posted online were also abundant. We're all underage, and we're all representing

Brazos High's Varsity Soccer team, and that kind of conduct is not allowed.

Coach made that very clear when he yelled at us this morning before our practice. We are examples of how student athletes should act, and that alcohol-fueled party was the exact opposite of what they expect from us. Now to make up for being such bad teenagers and poor role models, we're running laps.

I wasn't even at that stupid party. I don't drink, and I don't do drugs, and I'm actually a pretty good person as far as being a teenager goes. I might be the only junior at Brazos High who hasn't sent nude pictures of myself to anyone. I've never even *taken* a photo like that, much less sent it to someone.

But we are a team, and when one team member messes up, we all get punished as a team. Coach was also very adamant about that as well.

I look over at Brock Curtis as he jogs beside me and I scowl. Brock is always down for a wild house party with beer, booze, whatever. He's one of the people who should be punished right now. Not me.

It's only ten minutes until school starts when Coach finally lets us go back inside. We're all covered in sweat and have to shower before changing back into school clothes. The locker room is packed, and I have about three minutes to get dried off. My dark hair does not look good when it's wet. I let it grow out this summer and now it's just past my ears, but it's all shaggy and messy because I haven't had it trimmed since before school got out last year. I rake my fingers through it, but it's no use. Without a blow dryer, I look like a wet dog.

But it doesn't really matter, because I am the hottest guy in Brazos High School.

Trust me, I know how that sounds. Don't hate me—it's not my fault.

I didn't make up that title for myself. I don't even *believe* it, and that's the honest truth. But somewhere in junior high, girls started calling me cute. It's like I hit puberty and suddenly girls liked me. It only got worse in high school, when I got this reputation for being a player. I don't know who started the rumor, but people suddenly all believed that I dated college-aged girls and thought I was too good to date girls at my own school. I don't know. Then the freshman yearbook came out, and I was voted Hottest Freshman. And then last year I was voted Hottest Sophomore and Hottest Boy—for the entire student body. Now, as crazy as it sounds, being hot is kind of my identity.

And it's weird. It's *so* weird. All the guys act like it's some cosmic blessing to be crowned as a hot guy in high school, but I think it's more of a curse.

Girls are either intimidated by me or they think I'm some arrogant jerk who prides myself on looking good. No one knows my real secret, the embarrassing awful truth that I keep buried deep down inside...

I've never had a girlfriend.

Not even a date.

And now I'm seventeen years old, and a high school junior, and somehow I have this fan club of girls who look at me and bat their eyelashes in the hallways but never actually talk to me. And the longer I go without having a girlfriend, the more worried I get that I've been cursed with some kind of single-forever-life and that I'll never be able to break out of it and ask a girl out.

It really sucks.

The bell rings, meaning we have five minutes to get to class. The entire soccer team scrambles out of the locker room and toward the cafeteria to get our schedules. There's hardly anyone left in here, so I don't have to wait in line to get mine.

I have math class first period, which is way across the school and upstairs. Despite being forced to run laps for the last hour, I now have to run again to get to class on time.

"No running!"

I don't recognize the older woman who yells at me, but she looks like one of the teachers who would have no problem taking the time to write me up if I ignore her warning. So I slow down and give her a sheepish *please-don't-hate-me* smile as I walk by. Her stern expression turns soft and then she smiles back at me. That is probably the only benefit of being attractive. All women smile at me if I smile back at them. Of course, when an older woman does it, it's kind of creepy.

I ignore that thought and keep walking. Just great. Thanks to some idiots on my team, I'm going to be tardy on the first day of school. Awesome. What a wonderful way to start out the year.

"Hi, Jake."

I turn to see a pretty girl with blonde hair wave at me. I have no clue who she is, but I wave back. Every time a girl flirts with me I tell myself to just be brave and ask her on a date. But then I always chicken out. And it's not that I'm worried about being rejected... it's just that I don't want someone who only wants me for my looks.

I want to meet a girl in a fun casual way. I want to get to know her and slowly fall for her. I want her to do the same for me. But it feels like every girl at this school already knows me—if only for my reputation alone. They all see me and think "there goes the hottest guy in the school" and they don't even care to know who I am as a person.

The worst part is that every time I complain about my situation to my guy friends, they'll roll their eyes and make fake crying sounds and say, *"Oh boo-hoo, the hot guy is sad."*

Sometimes I daydream about waking up one day and becoming the actual jerk womanizing player that people assume I am. I imagine walking the halls with this weird superiority complex as if I think I'm better than everyone else because I was voted hottest guy in the school. I imagine just picking a random girl and asking her to be my girlfriend. I'm sure she would probably say yes. I mean, right? I'm the hottest guy in the school, after all.

But I can't do that. I don't want just any girl. I don't want someone who only wants me because they'll get bragging rights if they date me.

I want someone real. I want someone sweet. Maybe even someone who has no idea about my stupid reputation for being attractive.

This year, I don't want to continue being the single loser I am on the inside while looking like some kind of stud on the outside. This year, I am going to get a girlfriend. A real one.

THREE

Since my high school is a million years old, they decided to renovate it just before my freshman year, and then again over the summer. The Brazos High's Twitter page has been bragging about how we're a "technology school" now, and I wasn't sure what that meant exactly, but now it's obvious. As I shield my coffee from the crowded hallways, I can't help but notice the brightly flashing television screens all over the walls. There's a screen everywhere, and they're showing school announcements, stupid memes that I guess the administration thought were funny but aren't, and an ad to download the school's new app.

Our school has an app? Weird.

One thing I notice on the flashing screens are lots

and lots of student clubs to join this year. In addition to all the normal stuff like StuCo, there's also a sewing club, a swim club, and a manga club, among others. I've never been in a school club, but now they're starting to look like a really good idea. I should load up my schedule with clubs and activities because the busier I am, the less time I have to think about boys. It's a perfect plan.

I make my way down to the math hallway at the end of the school, keeping an eye on all the posters on the walls that advertise clubs so I can remember which ones I want to sign up for.

Between homework, clubs, and helping Abby babysit her three younger sisters, I should have no room at all in my life for thinking about boys. I definitely won't have any time to date one. And if there's no time to date, there's no time to think about them. It's the perfect plan.

I take a sip of my coffee and glance down at my schedule to find the exact room number of my first period class. I'm in room 1415 with Mr. Casey. I haven't heard of this teacher before, but I did just see something on the TV screens in the hallway that welcomed the fifteen new teachers our school hired this year. He must be one of them. I hope he's nice.

I'm not exactly bad at math, but I'm also not known for being good at it.

The two-minute warning bell chimes just as I walk in the door. Keeping with my promise to myself, I don't bother scanning the room to see who is in my class. I know Abby isn't in here, so no one else matters. Normally, the first day of school is exciting because you can check out your classmates and see if any cute guys will be in your classes. Abby and I used to love the first day of school because that's when you get to see who the new students are. It rarely happens, but occasionally some cute new guy would move to town over the summer and start school and then every girl in our grade would try to win him over.

It's so lame, I know.

I don't care about any of that anymore. I sit down at a desk near the back of the classroom. Every teacher arranges their desks differently, and this one has put us all in groups of two desks right next to each other. No one is sitting in the desk next to me, luckily.

"Good morning," I hear a man's voice say. I glance over—breaking my rule is okay if I'm just looking for the teacher—and see a younger man greeting students as they walk in. He's really young for a teacher—maybe mid-twenties? I don't know. But he's also wearing skinny khaki pants and a black T-shirt with some stupid math joke on it. His dirty blonde hair is longish on top and shaved on the sides and he has it all swooped over the top of his head and held in place with hair gel. He's definitely one of those hipster teachers who will probably try to be "cool" around us to win us over. I snort under my breath. I guess that's better than the drill sergeant algebra teacher I had last year who didn't allow cell phones or talking.

I sip my coffee, grateful that Mr. Casey isn't making us throw it away. Not every teacher was happy about the new coffee carts, and some make us toss the coffee at their door, but some let us keep it. Mr. Casey might not realize that letting us keep our coffees wins him way more bonus points than that dumb shirt he's wearing.

The bell rings and Mr. Casey flips off the lights, which really only turns off half the lights and leaves us bathed in a half-dim shadow. The Smartboard is on, and it's paused on the start of a YouTube video with the title: *So You're Lucky Enough to be in Mr. Casey's Class This Year*

Wow, my new teacher is a total dork.

"Welcome, welcome!" Mr. Casey says as he

walks up to the front of the class. I haven't seen him drinking any coffee, but wow is he energetic. He must have downed a whole pot of coffee before he got to school. "I'm so glad you're here. In case you didn't read your schedule, or this screen on the wall, or the various signs around the room—" He snorts as he points to a nameplate with his name on it that's been spelled out in rhinestones. "My name is Mr. Casey and I'm your math teacher this year. I am so, so glad to have you all, and we're going to learn a lot this year. We're going to have fun doing it, too."

He looks like he actually believes the words he says. Someone should tell him that math is not fun in any way, unless maybe if you're counting a bunch of money you just won or something. Still. He rambles on a bit, telling us about how he graduated with a Master's in Education at a much younger age than most people, and how he's worked a few years at a nearby high school but recently moved to Brazos, Texas to be close to his wife's family. At the mention of his wife, some of the girls audibly groan. Gross. I don't know why they would be crushing on a teacher. He's a teacher! Ew. Not to mention, boys of all kinds are stupid. And I'm so glad I've sworn them off this year.

In the half-shadows of our dimly lit room, I see two people rush into the classroom.

"Sorry," one of them says. He sounds a lot like a boy, so I don't bother looking over at him.

"No worries. I don't give out tardies on the first day of school," Mr. Casey says. "Have a seat, gentlemen. We're about to watch a video I put together, and I need to warn everyone that I graduated with an education degree—not a filmmaking one."

One of the guys who just walked in the classroom sits next to me. I hear him drop into the desk to my left, but even if I hadn't, I would know he's there because he smells really good. Like he just got out of the shower or something. He's all "mountain fresh" and shampoo smell. I swallow. I promised myself I wouldn't look at boys this year, but I should probably amend that promise to include not smelling them, either. Because smells can also be cute. I am so not in the mood for crushing on a guy. Not now, not ever.

After Mr. Casey's poorly filmed and edited video ends, I'm pretty sure I've heard more lame math jokes than anyone ever needs to hear in their lifetime. He turns the lights back on and then walks up to the front of the class. "I do things a little differently in my class. We aren't alone in this class. We're a team. And even more than that, we're partners.

You'll notice I've arranged the desks in groups of two," he says, holding out his hands toward us.

I do not like where this is going.

Mr. Casey looks very proud of himself though. "The person sitting next to you is your new partner for the school year. You will work together on all of your lessons. You will even take the exams together."

This makes a round of murmurs fill the room. Mr. Casey nods. "Yep. This is a teamwork class. Your partner is your responsibility as well as yourself. You will help each other and you will work together on everything. You will never be alone. Our principal hired me because of my teaching methods—and yeah, they're a little unconventional. But guess what? Life is unconventional. This plan of mine works, I promise. You will all have the highest math grade you've ever had in my class, and it's because of teamwork."

He claps his hands together in front of his chest. "So, with that said, please take a few minutes to meet your partner."

My heart pounds. Why did a guy sit next to me? Why, oh why, couldn't it have been a girl? Any girl. Even some mean girl. Or some girl with bad body odor. I don't care. Any girl in the world would have been better than this.

I turn to my left, and I wonder if maybe the Universe is playing some cruel cosmic joke on me right now.

Because the guy smiling at me—my new partner for the entire year—is Brazos High's Hottest Guy, Jake Johnson.

JAKE

Wow. I mean I know the Universe works in mysterious ways, but I have never seen it work like this—and so quickly, too. I want a girlfriend more than anything, and what happened? The Universe put me next to this beautiful girl who doesn't seem to care about me at all.

I know that might sound backward, but every time I sit next to a girl, they stare at me and smile at me and act all weird because of my reputation. This girl, whoever she is, hasn't looked at me once. It's like she couldn't care a single bit that I'm sitting next to her. It's refreshing.

And it's... hopeful?

I mean. I know it's stupid to fall for the first beautiful girl who doesn't care about me, so I should really slow down and stop daydreaming about asking this girl on a date.

Mr. Casey tells us to introduce ourselves to our new partner. I smile at her, and she looks over at me. And then it happens. I see it in her eyes.

She recognizes me.

Welp, I guess the Universe doesn't hand out totally perfect events.

"Hi," I say. "I'm Jake."

She lifts up her hand in a soft wave. "I'm Jules."

The classroom is filling with the chatter of everyone talking at once, and all the noise is actually helping to calm my nerves. I don't normally get nervous talking to girls, but there's something different about her. She has shoulder length brown hair and cute bangs that are crisply cut in a flat line above her eyebrows. I don't know many girls with bangs, but she really pulls off the hairstyle. She's sitting down, but I'm guessing she's pretty short, because everything about her is small. Maybe it's just the way she carries herself. She's all folded in, her hands in her lap as she leans forward in her desk.

"Are you cold?" I ask. "I have a jacket in my backpack."

Her face crumples in confusion. "No?" she says

with a look like I'm an idiot. "If anything, the coffee is making me warm."

"You looked cold," I say. Wow, I am lame. The lamest of the lame. Like, it doesn't get any lamer than this.

"So are you good at math?" Jules asks. She takes a sip of her coffee. "Please tell me you're good at math."

"I'm going to college for mechanical engineering," I say. "That's how good at math I am."

Her eyes widen, then she looks down at her coffee cup. "Awesome. I'm not bad at math but I'm no math genius, either. I'll try not to let you down this year."

"Nah, I think we'll be fine," I say, glancing at the desks in front of us where two of our school's biggest stoners are sitting. "We'll definitely do better than they will."

She smiles. "I think that trashcan in the corner of the room will get better grades than those guys," she whispers.

We've only been talking a few moments, and yet Jules feels so different from other girls in my grade. She's talking to me like I'm normal. Like I don't have some stupid popularity reputation about me. I like it. I wish everyone treated me this normally.

"I also have a lot of free time," Jules says while her gaze goes right back to her coffee cup. "So I'll be able to study a lot to catch up to your level."

Mr. Casey is walking by, and he stops short when he overhears Jules. "There will be no individual studying," he says, tapping his hand on her desk with each word. Then he looks out over at the entire class. "Guys, this is a partnership. Everything you do for my class will be with your partner. No solo studying, no solo math work."

"Both me and my partner don't have a car," someone says from across the room. "How are we supposed to study together every single day?"

"This is the modern world," Mr. Casey says, continuing on his slow walk around the room. "We live in the future. You all have smart phones and Snapchat and Facetime. You kids are already on your phones all day, every day. Make it work. I am not joking when I say you will do everything with your partner this year. Your grade will be your partner's grade. Your partner's grade will be yours. If your partner gets the flu and misses school for a week, you might as well get the flu too because you'll be doing everything together."

Maria Estevan's hand shoots up in the air. "Sir, you better call my mom and tell her that you're making me talk to my partner because she grounds me from my phone like once a week."

Mr. Casey chuckles. "I'm happy to talk to any parents who need clarification."

He answers a few more questions, and then he starts passing out a packet of worksheets stapled together. Mine lands on my desk with a heavy thunk. It must be at least twenty pages of math problems. I flip through the papers. It's mostly stuff we learned last year, so I guess he wants to see what level we're all at. I'm all for easy first day of school work, but twenty pages is a lot.

"This packet is due at the end of the week," Mr. Casey announces as he finishes walking around the room, passing out papers. A collective sigh of relief fills the classroom. Twenty pages over a week is no big deal. In one class period? It would have been awful.

Jules writes her name at the top of her work-sheet. Then, underneath it, she writes my name. There's this weird little pitter patter thing going on in my chest when I see her do it. She glances over at me and shrugs. "I figure he'll want both of our names on everything."

"Good call," I say, writing her name on my own packet.

Mr. Casey finishes answering everyone's questions about his weird teaching method, and then he plays music over the speakers that he's set up in the corner of each room. That's another thing other teachers don't do. I wonder if it's also part of his "unconventional method" of teaching. Jules and I get to work, and we talk quietly to each other while we work out the problems on the page. She's actually much smarter than she made it sound like because she knows this stuff just as well as I do. We work through several pages, completing more than we need to seeing as how this packet has to last us for the entire week. Jules and I work together really well, and she's both smart and sweet in this way that makes my chest constrict. Deep down, I know I shouldn't be crushing on my math partner. It's only the first day of school, and a crush like this could totally derail me for the entire school year, especially if she doesn't like me back. After all, she probably has a boyfriend. She's way too pretty to be single.

"I think we did too much work," Jules says after we finish a problem on differential equations. "We're already on page ten. Oops."

"Maybe he'll let us sleep at our desks if we finish early. I could really use it after coach's training torture that's going to last all week."

Jules slides her packet into the inside folder of her binder. "What sport do you play?"

I stare at her in stunned silence for a second. Does she really not know? I thought everyone knew what sport I played. "Soccer," I say. "Did you just move here?"

She gives me a look like I'm an idiot. "No..."

And now I really feel like an idiot. "I've just never seen you before," I say, because telling her that the simple fact she doesn't know what sport I play is weird would be the worst thing to say right now.

"I've seen you," she says, but she's not looking at me. She hasn't looked at me much this morning, which is also unusual. I don't try to be arrogant or anything, but girls usually stare at me so much that it's annoying. Jules puts her binder into her backpack. "I think the whole school knows you. You're popular. I'm just some random girl."

My instinct is to tell her that she's not some random girl, but is actually one of the most beautiful girls I've ever seen. Luckily, I'm smart enough to shut up that part of my brain.

"I'm really glad I sat next to you," I say over the commotion of everyone else packing up their stuff because the bell is about to ring. "I could have been stuck with a terrible partner."

She laughs. "Same."

If I wasn't such a total and complete loser, and if she wasn't my math partner for the year, I'd ask for her number. Or I'd ask her on a date. Yet, she is my partner, and I am a loser, and I'm sitting here feeling like this is the biggest missed opportunity in the world. Jules seems perfect. I'd love to get to know her better.

Then it hits me. All the stuff Mr. Casey talked about earlier comes back to me. I hold out my phone. "Hey, we should probably exchange numbers or Snapchat names or something. You know, for Mr. Casey's rules."

"Oh," she says, looking startled. "Sure. Totally."

It's not exactly the way I'd hoped to get a girl's number this year. And it's not exactly romantic, either, when she writes down her number and Snapchat handle on a scrap piece of paper. She's all business-like, giving me her info because we're math partners.

But still, when the bell rings and I tell her goodbye and she smiles at me, I can't help but feel like maybe... just maybe... something good is happening.

FIVE

JULES

Abby hangs her hand out the passenger window of my car. "You getting a car is the greatest thing to happen to us this year," she says wistfully, closing her eyes as the wind whips through her long hair.

"Okay, that's a bit dramatic," I say with a snort. "But it is accurate. Now move over, I'm rolling up the windows."

"Blah, you're no fun," Abby says.

"I don't want my hair getting all messed up," I say in return as I roll up the windows. It actually looks halfway cute today. My bangs were cooperating, which is basically unheard of, and I want them to stay nice so I can just dry shampoo my hair in the morning and not have to fix them again.

Now that I can officially drive, I don't have to ride the bus to Abby's house anymore, and she won't have to ride the bus to mine. We live only a few blocks away from each other, which puts us on the same school bus. The driver knows us well enough now to let us get off at each other's houses, even though that's technically against the rules without a parent note.

Now, we don't need notes. We have wheels.

I pull up to Abby's house right as our former school bus stops in front of it. Abby has three little sisters and they all pile out of the bus.

"Not fair!" Maria says, crossing her arms over her chest. "We have to ride the stupid bus and you get to ride with Jules? That is so not fair."

"Yeah it is," Abby says, rolling her eyes. "When you're in high school you can bum rides off your friends."

We head inside to the mouth-watering smell of Abuela's tamales. Abby and her sisters live with her dad's mom while her parents are in Mexico helping out her mom's parents who are both in failing health. It's already been a year that her parents have been gone, and I think Abby has felt really pressured to take up the role of guardian and boss while they're away. That's because Abuela is just way too nice.

She doesn't discipline Abby's sisters, and they're all pretty obnoxious girls between the ages of eight and thirteen.

That's why we lock ourselves in Abby's bedroom when we hang out, so the girls can't annoy us. Sorry, not sorry.

"I really wish my parents would get back," Abby says as she tosses her backpack on her bed and then plugs her phone into the charger by her nightstand. "But then I feel terrible saying that, because they basically won't come back until my grandparents die and don't need them anymore, and ugh, what kind of horrible person am I?"

"You can want your parents back and also not want your grandparents to die," I say. It sounds a little morbid, but I mean it in a nice way. "It's okay to be stressed out."

She sighs and blows the hair out of her face. "I know. I'm just tired of being stressed out. Seems like everything I do is for my sisters or Abuela and not for me."

"Well, I have a car now, so let's do something this weekend. Whatever you want."

Abby frowns. "I have to babysit this weekend."

Abuela's one vice is Saturday night bingo down at the VFW hall.

"Bummer," I say. "Maybe Sunday?"

"Church," Abby says.

"I mean after church." She goes to mass every Sunday morning but is usually home by noon.

She shakes her head. "Abuela volunteered me to help set up the booths for the festival next weekend. My whole weekend is shot."

I didn't realize my best friend was so stressed out lately. I guess I haven't really been around much this summer. I spent most of my days being mopey and heartbroken and she put up with all of it. It's time for me to be a better friend.

"I'll come over and help you babysit," I say. "I'll bring junk food and we'll binge watch cheesy romance movies."

"You sure?" Abby says. "You hate romance movies."

"No...I temporarily hated them this summer. I'm good now."

Abby gives me a side-eyed look.

"I swear I'm all better now!"

"Just last week you were dreading going back to school because you might see you-know-who," she says, whispering that last part as if Trevor's name was Voldemort.

I shrug. "I'm over it. My heart was broken, but

I'm all good now. I decided to dedicate myself to school, and to my friends, and to like, join clubs and stuff."

Abby's expression is one hundred percent skeptical and it makes me laugh. "I'm serious!" I say.

"Okay, well I believe you. But only because you're my best friend and I know you wouldn't lie to me."

She turns on her television and we lay across her bed to begin watching our favorite show, a witty comedy that we've seen a million times, while we talk about our classes. I don't mention my first period math class. I'm still not quite recovered from what happened today. I spent all fifty minutes of class chatting with Jake freaking Johnson as if we were friends or something. It was weird. And he is so, *so* hot. Not that it matters.

My phone is on the bed next to Abby's phone, and they're both positioned right between us while we watch TV. When the familiar beep of a new Snapchat message fills the air, we both look over because it could be from either one of our phones. But mine is the one lighting up.

"Oh. My. God," Abby says, eyes so wide they look like golf balls. "Jake Johnson just Snapped you? What!?"

I grab my phone and try really, really hard to act like it's no big deal. "He's my math partner," I say, opening his message.

———————————

Did you get Mr. Casey's email?

———————————

"Jake Johnson!" Abby says while I type out a reply.

———————————

No? I'll check it now.

———————————

"Jake Johnson."

I look up at Abby. "Stop repeating his name. It's not a big deal."

"It is a huge deal," she says, slapping my arm several times in a row like she just can't contain herself. "He's the—"

"—Hottest guy in school, I know." I roll my eyes. "For being such a player, he's actually kind of a nerd at math."

"WHY. IS. HE. MESSAGING. YOU?" Abby says.

"Our teacher is insane and he's making us partner up with someone and work with them all year." I tell myself if I act like it's no big deal, maybe I'll actually believe it. Because, no matter how quiet I've been all day, internally, I'm kind of freaking out about being Jake's partner. After first period was over, I had three girls confront me in the hallway about how jealous they were or how they wanted to switch partners with me. It was weird and also strangely exhilarating.

I check my school email and see a message from my math teacher, which was sent out to everyone. He gave us a link to a Google form that's a bunch of random questions. He wants us to fill out the answers twice. Once for ourselves, and other time with what we think our partner would answer.

I open my Snapchat app and reply to Jake.

What kind of crap assignment is this?

---

lol, right? Here are all my answers so you can cheat. Maybe get a couple of them wrong on purpose so it doesn't look like cheating.

---

maybe this is a trick? Maybe he wants us to have the perfect answers so it proves we "worked together" like he wants us to do?

You're right..... that might be it. Let's do perfect answers. Will you send me yours?

sure thing

I look up from my phone and see my best friend staring at me, her jaw hanging open. "How on earth are you just lying there texting Jake freaking Johnson as if it's nothing?"

I roll my eyes. "You know, I'm pretty sure his middle name isn't *freaking*."

Now Abby rolls her eyes. "I'm just stunned, that's all. My best friend is now friends with the most popular and hottest guy in school. That makes me like...secondhand popular myself."

I snort out a laugh.

Abuela calls for us from the kitchen, saying the tamales will be ready in ten minutes. Normally, the sound of Abuela's amazing cooking is the greatest thing I can hear all day. But right now, I'm barely thinking about the tamales...

I'm thinking about Jake.

And how I have a screenshot of all his answers to this stupid survey thing. They're kind of personal questions, too. Why am I suddenly eager to see what his answers are? It shouldn't matter.

"I should probably go," I say, making an exaggerated frown. "Our teacher just assigned a lot of work that's due tomorrow."

"Can't you stay for dinner?" Abby asks, pausing the TV.

It's a reasonable question. Dinner is almost ready, after all, and Abuela's tamales are to die for.

But something weird happens to my entire body, because suddenly I don't understand what I'm saying. I'm shaking my head and looking sad and lying to my best friend.

"Sorry, it's important. I wish I could stay but I should really get home."

Abby walks me to the front door, and the smell of a delicious dinner that I'm totally abandoning follows us as well. I can't believe I'm ditching out on my best friend just to get home and read through Jake's answers. But I'm so eager to see what he has to say that I can't help myself.

Something is seriously wrong with me.

SIX

JAKE

It's not weird to add your math partner on Instagram. At least, that's what I tell myself. She's pretty easy to find because her Instagram username is the same as her Snapchat. Mr. Casey wants us to stay in constant contact, after all, so that's what I'm doing. At least that's my excuse.

I scroll through Jules' account and look at her pictures. She spends a lot of time with her best friend, Abby Pena, who is a girl I vaguely know from the two years I took American Sign Language class in junior high. Jules doesn't have many other pictures of herself on her profile, but she does post pictures of her cat occasionally. It's cute. I wish there were more pictures of herself, though. I want to roll my eyes at how pathetically pathetic I'm being. Here I am dying to look at her beautiful face on the small screen of my phone. It's official – I'm crushing hard. This should be easy for me. I should be able to pick out a girl I like and ask her to be my girlfriend. Instead, I'm lying on my bed after school, stalking her Insta like I'm some kind of creep.

The app has a new notification. I click on it and then sit up in bed. Jules just followed me back. Sweet.

We spent the first week of school just being Snapchat friends, which wasn't as fun because she never posts anything to her account.

Now we're Snapchat *and* Instagram friends. If I can't get the courage to flirt with her in person, maybe I'll get the courage to flirt with her online. I can't believe it's been an entire week and I've only talked about math with Jules. I want to talk about better things than math. Like topics that include if she likes me or not.

I also don't want to be weird about it.

I'm scrolling through my Instagram page, looking at my newest posts and wondering if Jules will like any of them now that she's following me back. It's so weird but in a refreshing way that she didn't already follow me. We have two thousand students at Brazos

High and I have five thousand followers. Pretty much everyone already follows me, but she didn't.

I both love and hate that fact. For one, maybe she's not obsessed with me like other girls are. Maybe she could get to know the real me and get to like me as Jake Johnson, regular guy. Not Jake Johnson, hottest guy in school.

But on the other hand… if she didn't follow me already, maybe she doesn't like me at all. Maybe I'm not her type. And that would really, really suck.

I lazily watch TV for half an hour and constantly refresh my app, but Jules never likes any of my recent Instagram photos. I decide to post a new photo. Something that makes me look good, but not like I'm trying too hard.

"Dex!" I call out. Within a few seconds, our cat Dexter comes rushing into my room. He's solid white with blue eyes and he's totally adorable. I tap my shoulder and he leaps up onto it, which is his favorite trick to do. With Dexter perched on my shoulder like some kind of parrot, I take a selfie of us and post it to Instagram.

Now I wait.

"So let me get this straight," Oliver says while we jog laps around the high school on Friday morning. "You want a girl to like you so you posted a random photo that has nothing to do with her and she didn't like it and now you're all upset about it?"

I keep my gaze focused ahead of me as we jog. "Yeah... It sounds stupid when you say it like that."

"That's because it is stupid." Oliver snorts. "Dude, you're worrying over nothing. Just ask her out. You of all people shouldn't worry about getting rejected."

Of all my team mates, I'd say Oliver is my closest friend. But even he doesn't know my secret. Even he thinks I've dated several girls over the years. He, like everyone else, just thinks I keep my love life under wraps and that I don't brag about the girls I date. So although I've told him about my crush on Jules, he can't see why this is such a big deal. He has no idea that I've never had a girlfriend.

We turn around the east corner of the school and keep jogging. It's still sticky and warm this morning but at least it's not raining like it was yesterday.

"She's different from other girls," I say. "She's not like... obsessed with me."

"Oh poor you," Oliver says sarcastically. "A girl isn't obsessed with you..."

"Dude, I'm being serious. With most girls, it's obvious they like me. With her... I don't know. She's nice to me in class but she doesn't seem to care about me outside of class."

"Maybe she has a boyfriend."

I shake my head. "She's single."

The survey Mr. Casey had us fill out on the first day of school told me that. Jules is single, sixteen years old, loves the color purple, and hates butter on her popcorn. She's also allergic to maple syrup. I don't know what Mr. Casey was trying to do with those surveys that were completely unrelated to math, but I'm glad he did them. I got to learn more about this girl and it only made me crush on her harder.

"I don't know what to tell you, man." Oliver's breath is ragged because he spent most of the summer break in Aruba with his parents than at home practicing soccer like the rest of us. "You're a good-looking guy, and you're nice. Just ask her out, man."

It's easier said than done, but I'm not about to let him know that. I nod. "Yeah, I will."

After showering in the locker room, I head into class feeling an overwhelming sense of urgency. It's Friday, which means if I don't make a connection with Jules today, I'll have to go the entire weekend before I see her again. I take a deep breath as I walk in the classroom. It's now or never.

Jules is sitting at her desk right next to mine. Her headphones are in and she's bobbing her head to whatever music she's listening to. Dang. I can't talk to her now. I sit down and take out my math notebook. Mr. Casey warns us that today will be filled with note-taking, and the entire class grumbles about it.

When the bell rings signaling the start of class, Jules puts her music away and I look over at her.

"Good morning," I say.

"Morning," she says back. She's also taking out her notebook, so she doesn't even look at me when she says it, and it crushes my soul a bit. I'm not used to girls not looking at me.

As the class goes on, I'm having the hardest time paying attention to Mr. Casey's lesson, and although I write out everything he does in my notebook, it doesn't make any sense. It's all just numbers and symbols. My mind is focused on Jules and how she smells like vanilla and coffee and how those are my two favorite scents now. I want her to like me, and I've never had to worry about this type of thing before. I guess this is what my friends feel like when they crush on a girl who doesn't like them back.

A few minutes before class is over, Mr. Casey drops a stack of papers on the podium at the front of the class. "Right Partners, come get two of these," he says. That's a thing he does—since the desks are set up into groups of two, he calls one of the desks the Right Partner, and the other side the Left Partner. He alternates who has to get up to get papers or turn them in. Jules gets up and walks to the front of the class, grabbing our new set of worksheets.

When she walks back, Julio Perez is too busy flirting with the girl sitting behind him to notice Jules. He jumps backward while doing some stupid dance move thing and knocks right into Jules, knocking her off her feet.

I reach out to catch her, and everything happens so fast. In a split second, Jules has fallen into my arms, knocking into the desk and landing in my lap. Jules is in my lap. I repeat: *Jules is in my lap.*

"You okay?" I ask, loosening my arms from around her waist. It goes against everything in me because I want to hold on tightly, but I also don't want to be a creep.

Her eyes are wide and frightened, and she grabs

her hip, wincing. "Yeah. I think your desk bruised me, though."

"Sorry," I say with a frown. "Nice one, Julio."

"My bad," he says, giving Jules a guilty look before turning back to the girl he's flirting with. What a jerk.

"It's fine," Jules says. She rubs her hip and looks over at me. "If you didn't catch me I'd probably have bashed my head on the floor, so thanks."

"Hey, that's what math partners are for," I say with a laugh. She smiles at me. My heart turns to mush.

Then she blinks, as if she's just realized something. "Sorry, I'll get off you," she says, scrambling to her feet just as the bell rings and everyone else rushes toward the door, preventing me from saying anything. But that's probably for the best, because I'm not sure what I'd say anyway. I'm too stuck in the daydream of how good it felt to have her in my arms.

When I told the universe I wanted a girlfriend, I didn't expect the perfect girl to fall, quite literally, into my lap.

But I'm so glad she did.

SEVEN

JULES

Dear Universe:

Why do you do this to me? I spent all week trying not to think about Jake and how cute he is and how badly I wish I could crush on him and then you literally threw me into his lap! That's not cool, Universe.

Not cool at all.

Love,

Jules

My cheeks flush red as soon as I walk into class on Monday morning. Turns out an entire weekend of babysitting with your best friend does not erase the warm, mushy feelings you get when you remember falling into the lap of the hottest guy you've ever seen. Holy cow. I mean, what?? How did that happen? Why did that happen? I was doing perfectly fine at ignoring him until stupid Julio made me fall into Jake's arms.

Now he's all I think about.

I take a deep breath and let it out slowly. My coffee trembles in my hand. I've only had one sip of it since I bought it from the coffee cart. My stomach is all tight with anxiety and I can't seem to drink. I'm about to see him again. After a weekend of trying not to think about him, he's about to be right here in my class, sitting next to me. I'm not sure I can survive forty-five minutes of being so close to him now that I've sat in his lap. It was hard enough to ignore him before that little incident. Now, it'll be a monumental task.

With shaky legs, I make my way to my desk and set my coffee down so I don't spill it.

"Morning," Jake says. He says it every day. And every day, the sound of his cute voice sends a little shiver down my spine.

"Morning," I croak back as I drop into my seat.

The only reprieve I got last Friday was that Mr. Casey didn't assign any weekend homework, so Jake and I didn't have to talk at all. Now, it's the start of a new week and I'm sure he'll have us doing something together. Here's hoping I can get through it without making a fool of myself. This year was supposed to be about *not* thinking of boys, and I didn't even make it one whole day.

The Universe really has some explaining to do. I don't think I've done anything to deserve this kind of treatment. I'm a good person. Why is life torturing me like this?

Mr. Casey gives his lesson, which includes playing several YouTube videos with math tutorials. Normally I like the days where we watch videos, but today, with the lights turned off and the glow of the Smartboard making Jake's side profile look extra sexy, I wish we could go back to regular boring classwork.

I am hyper aware of Jake sitting next me. I notice when he moves or when he sighs, or when his pencil lead breaks and he has to click the tip of his mechanical pencil to fix it. I used to like crushing on guys, but now it's just all heartache.

I told myself not to think about guys this year and now I've totally ruined it. Not cool.

Mr. Casey turns the lights back on and elaborates about an equation we just saw in the last video. He uses different colored dry erase markers to write out different parts of the problem, but every time he uses the green one, I can't read what he writes because it's too light on the white board. I usually lean over and ask Jake what it says. He must have superior vision because he doesn't have a problem reading Mr. Casey's green writing. This time, when the green marker emerges, Jake slides his paper over onto my desk, so I can see it. Then he writes out exactly what Mr. Casey puts on the board.

"Thanks," I whisper.

"Always," he whispers back.

My heart pounds. I hate it. And I like it. But I mostly hate it.

This is not good! Stop crushing on him! It doesn't matter that he's totally hot. It doesn't matter that he's so considerate he remembers that I can never read the green marker and he proactively let me copy his paper. None of it matters. Because underneath all of that, he's still just a guy. And I have sworn off guys this year.

I rest my head on my hand and let my hair fall in front of my face, blocking him from my peripheral vision. It helps a little, pretending he's not there.

Now I know why all the girls swoon over Jake Johnson. Everything about him is cute. I guess I can't blame the entire boy-liking population of Brazos High for swooning over him. I just wish I was immune to it all.

Mr. Casey turns off the lights again. "One more video before class is over." He grins like he's the coolest dude ever. "I think you will like this one."

What plays next is an ultra dorky rap video made by some extraordinarily dorky math guys who think they're funny trying to teach educational stuff in a rap. This might work on third graders, but here in high school, it's totally lame.

I start packing up my stuff into my backpack, and my pencil rolls off my desk. In the dark, I lean over to get it. My hand touches another hand. I jump and see Jake smiling at me, his hand over my pencil. He sits up and gives it to me.

"Thanks," I mumble. My skin is scorching hot from where my fingertips grazed his.

"Always," he whispers back. His eyes sparkle in the glow of the Smartboard and my heart does this little mini seizure in my chest. I swallow, but it doesn't help anything.

I know this is math class, not science, but I just learned a very scientific truth:

That whole cliché about feeling sparks between two people? It's true.

It's so, very, true.

EIGHT

JAKE

I THINK I FOUND THE PERFECT THING TO distract me from thinking about Jules and how I'm such a pathetic sack of pathetic-ness for not being able to ask her out. That thing is my two year old brother, Geoffrey. My parents decided to go out to see their favorite rock band perform tonight, on a Tuesday of all nights, and they left me to babysit. My brother is cute and all when he's clean and laughing, but for extended periods of time, he's a total handful. My parents are going all the way to Houston, which is a three hour drive, so they leave the second I get home from school.

Normally I'd complain about this and ask for money to order a pizza or something to make up for this huge inconvenience. But I'm cool with it tonight, because there's no way I'll be able to think about Jules while I'm caring for my energetic little brother. I set up his favorite toys in the living room and then I turn on a kid movie that he's only seen a million times instead of the ones he's seen two million times, and it keeps him entertained while I work on my homework. I only have a few things to do for my other classes, and I finish quickly, leaving only math work.

Mr. Casey gave us another stack of worksheets and they're not due until Friday, so Jules and I don't have to work on it today. In fact, it'll be good if we don't work on it today. I need a day to just clear my mind. Last night when I wasn't able to sleep (because I was thinking of her) I started searching online for ways to get over being too scared to ask a girl out. One very interesting article said you should distance yourself from your crush so you can gain some perspective. To recharge, if you will. It said spending too much time around them will only make you crazy and then you'll be too nervous to ask them out. I have no idea if that random person on the internet knew what they were talking about when they wrote that article, but I'm going to try it out.

My Snapchat app lights up. I nearly choke on my soda. Just a few seconds after I told myself not to message Jules today—she messaged me. I glance at my brother and make sure he's still happily watching the TV and not getting into trouble, and then I read her message.

It's a picture of her math worksheets, with the words: *Wanna do this tonight or later?*

The cheesy grin on my face is so cheesy it's actually making my cheeks hurt. I get on the floor and sit next to Geoffrey and take a picture of the two of us. Geoffrey loves pictures and he always smiles really big for them. I write: *I'm babysitting tonight so I might not be any good at math*

Jules immediately sends back a picture of her face. Her hand is covering her mouth in what is clearly an "aww" expression that mirrors the caption she types over the photo: *AWW! OMG HE'S SO CUTE! Is that your brother?*

I wish Snapchat didn't erase photos right after you receive them because I'd love to look back at that one. She looked so happy. And so incredibly beautiful.

I reply with another photo of us and the caption: *Yep.*

I guess our homework can wait, she says using the text function on Snapchat. *I'm jealous though, because I love kids! Tell your parents I will babysit for them!*

I bite my lip. The first reply I think of is kind of totally inappropriate so I can't say it—*do you want to babysit me or my brother?* My cheeks flush at the very thought of saying it. But then I think of a better reply. After all, this is the perfect opportunity to spend time with her outside of being in Mr. Casey's class. So what if that online article told me to stay away from her until I wasn't nervous... I want to see her.

I take another selfie and send her it with the caption: *you're welcome to come hang out with us!*

Her reply comes three minutes later, and it's the longest three minutes in the world. I must be in some kind of time warp caused by the impatience of waiting on a beautiful girl, but eventually she does reply.

Sounds fun! What's your address?

Geoffrey is the first one to rush out the door when Jules arrives. "Hi!" he says, waving his chubby toddler hand at her.

"Hello," Jules says, kneeling down so that she's on his eye level. "What's your name?"

"Geoffrey," he says. His fingers go straight to his

mouth—he always does that when he's nervous. *I'm nervous too, little brother. I'm so nervous.*

"It's nice to meet you, Geoffrey," she says, smiling at him. "My name is Jules."

Jules looks just like always, but she's somehow different now that we're not at school. She's wearing black Adidas track pants with flip flops and a pale pink shirt. It's casual and yet so very cute on her.

I lead Jules through my house and to the back yard where we have a nice patio setup. My parents love hosting parties to watch football, so there's ceiling fans, a TV, music, and an outdoor kitchen out here, as well as our swimming pool.

"Whoa," Jules says, looking around in awe. "Your backyard is awesome."

"Yeah, it's my parent's favorite part of the house, and it's not even technically in the house," I say. "But it's nice to study out here."

She slides her backpack off her shoulders and we sit at the patio table. I put Geoffrey in his favorite swing which hangs from the patio ceiling and I give him some picture books to play with. He likes to play with his books and pretend like he's "studying" whenever I'm studying.

Jules and I get a decent amount of work done before Geoffrey gets bored and starts asking to get out of his swing. I pick him up and put him in my lap, then look back at our worksheets. "Looks like we finished just in time because this little guy will probably need a nap soon."

"No nap!" my brother says, balling up his little fists in defiance. But then he yawns and Jules and I both laugh.

"I love naps," Jules says. "I wish I could take a nap."

"Me too," I say, nodding enthusiastically. Geoffrey hates naps and it's always a struggle to get him to lay down, but my mom wants me to keep him on his daily routine, so he'll need a nap even if he doesn't want one. "Come on, little dude," I say, standing up and reaching out my hand for his. "Let's walk Jules to her car."

"This was fun," Jules says as we walk up to the front yard. "Thanks for inviting me over."

She grins at me as we walk and it makes my knees weak. She seems genuinely happy, and like she really did have a good time hanging out with me. Plus, she didn't have to. Our work could have been done at our separate houses, with occasional Snapchat messages between us like usual. But she came over, and she hung out with me. Maybe she likes me, too.

I know I'll never get the courage to ask her to be my girlfriend if I don't find the courage to ask her on a date. We stop in front of her car. She takes her car keys out of her pocket and then accidentally drops them. My little brother bends down and picks them up for her.

"Thank you," she says, beaming at him. She ruffles his hair.

"Are you going bye-bye?" Geoffrey asks, one finger in his mouth.

"Yep, I'm going home to take a nap," Jules says, winking up at me. "Naps are so much fun."

My brother shakes his head. "I hate naps!"

"That's too bad," Jules says. "I think naps are cool."

My little brother stares at her, almost as if he's trying to figure out why she thinks naps are cool. The little gears in his toddler mind are spinning—I think she might actually make him want to take a nap now, if only to see why she thinks they're so cool.

"Your brother is the cutest," Jules tells me. She clicks the unlock button on her key fob. Then she looks back at him. "If you take a nap today, I'll bring you a present next time I come over."

Geoffrey's eyes widen. "Okay!"

I might be grinning bigger than he is though,

because Jules just said she'd come over again. That has to be a good sign. "Hey," I say, telling myself to hurry up and spit out the words before I lose my nerve. "Oliver is having a party at his house on Friday. It'll be mostly the soccer team and our friends. Do you want to go with me?"

"Sure," she says. "Sounds fun."

I grin. I want to hug her. But that would be weird, right? Probably.

"Cool," I say, reminding myself that I'm Jake Johnson, and I shouldn't be nervous. I should have expected her to say yes. "See you at school tomorrow."

NINE

As much as I try to play this off like it's nothing, my thoughts are a hurricane of Jake. I can't just sit here and be normal and not think about him anymore. Because things have changed... Jake and I aren't just "see each other in class" friends now... we are friends who will hang out at a soccer party this Friday.

Maybe I'm overthinking this.

We are still just *friends* after all. So maybe it's not a big deal.

The microwave beeps and Abby reaches up and takes out our bowl of queso. She stirs it with a chip and then takes a bite. "Hmm," she says as she chews. "It should be a little hotter." She places it back in the microwave then turns to me, putting a hand on her hip. "So what's been up with you and your math partner?"

"Funny you should mention him..." I say. I pull out the barstool next to the kitchen island and take a seat. "I think he asked me to a party..."

"You *think?* Or he did?" Abby says, eyes wide as she waits for my answer, as if whatever I say next is a life or death sort of situation.

I shrug. "He said there's a soccer party at Oliver's house and he asked if I wanted to go."

"With him?" Abby shrieks. "Like a date!"

I shake my head. "No... it's not a date... but he invited me to a soccer party and those guys are popular. So... I guess I'm being invited to popular stuff now?"

The microwave beeps and Abby takes out our queso. This time the temperature passes her chip taste test. She pushes the bag of chips toward me as we hover around the kitchen island with our junk food.

"How did he say it?" Abby asks over a mouthful of queso. "Like... what were the words he used?"

I roll my eyes. "No. No way. I'm not going down this rabbit hole with you where we over analyze everything that happened with a boy. This is nothing. He doesn't like me and I don't like him. We will not be talking about this anymore."

Abby groans. "I think he might like you, though! He's always Snapchatting you!"

"That's because we're always talking about school work. That's it, nothing else. It's not like he tells me good morning and good night each day or anything."

"Maybe he's just waiting to make his move," she says, wiggling her eyebrows.

I give her a look. "No, he's not. We are just school friends. End of discussion."

Abby dips a chip into the queso then points it at me. "Okay, fine. Here's the deal: if he picks you up and drives you to that party, it's a date. If he doesn't, then it's not a date and I'll totally drop it."

She makes a good point, but I'm not going to admit that. Jake and I didn't talk about how we'd get to this party on Friday... I just said I would go. A flutter of nervous energy rises up in my stomach as I think about it.

The very next day, I'm still thinking about it as I walk into first period. Jake tells me good morning like he always does, and I say it back to him like I always do, and then Mr. Casey passes out our first big exam. We have to do the exams with our partners, so Jake and I murmur to each other all class period, but there's no spare time to chat about anything else. The bell rings about five seconds after we turn in our tests. Mr. Casey pulled out all the stops on this test... it was hard. Jake is incredible at math and we still had several problems we had to work out a few times to get the answers. Something tells me our teacher did that on purpose to make us work harder with our partners.

I'm walking out of class when I hear Jake call my name. "Wait up," he says as he jogs down the hallway to catch up with me.

Every girl in our vicinity is looking at him. And at me, for walking with him. How does he put up with this kind of attention?

"What's up?" I say.

"I need your address."

"Why?" I ask. More looks come our way from girls walking by us. They're clearly trying to eavesdrop on our conversation. "Are you putting me on your Christmas card list?"

He grins. "No, for the party on Friday. I figure I'll get you around eight? We don't want to get there too early and look like losers."

I swallow. Abby is going to freak. I might actually freak. He wants to pick me up and drive me to this party. That makes it sort of a date? Oh no. No, no, no. I can't date anyone this year and I certainly can't date Jake. All I have to do is remind myself how Trevor broke my heart over social media and I'll snap back to reality and remember why I promised myself I wouldn't date. Boys are not worth it.

But I also want to go to this party. It could be a fun thing to do. And doing fun things was part of my plan for this year, so long as those fun things don't involve dating boys...

"I actually live way across town," I say even though I know for a fact that I live about two blocks away from Jake since I went to his house the other day. "I'll just meet you at the party so you're not driving out of the way."

He frowns. "Are you sure? I don't mind."

"Yeah, I'll just meet you there." I grin up at him like it's no big deal and like I'm not freaking out at all.

"Uh, okay," he says, his lips pressing into a line. Is he... disappointed? I can't tell.

He nods at me. "See you tomorrow."

TEN

JAKE

HIP HOP PLAYS LOUDLY THROUGH THE Bluetooth speaker in Oliver's game room. Some guys from my team are battling it out over a game of air hockey while others stand around the dartboard or play pool. Oliver's parents are well off and that makes his house the best one for these parties. My parents would never let me throw a party with more than maybe five people at my house.

My phone lights up with a text from Jules.

I'm here... so do I just walk in? I have no idea how soccer parties work, lol.

I grin at how cute she is, and then write back.

I'll meet you at the door.

Jules smiles at me when I open Oliver's front door and see her standing there, hands in her pockets. She seems nervous, and it makes me realize that I can't remember the first house party I went to. Is this her first time? I've just kind of always been part of the popular crowd since junior high. People invite me to every party, even if I don't want to go. Jules is kind of quiet at school. Maybe she doesn't get invited to a lot of parties. Maybe she's more of a homebody than a party girl. The idea of spending a weekend curled up with her on the couch sounds so much better than being at a party.

"Hey," I say. I tell her hi every single day at school, but it feels different now that we're at a house party and not in our assigned seats in Mr. Casey's classroom.

"I'll be honest," she says, biting on her bottom lip. "I don't think I know many people here. I'm not even sure why I came? I guess I'm trying to be cool."

Oh my gosh, this girl is adorable. I grin. "Come on, I'll show you around."

I let Jules into Oliver's house and introduce her to some of the guys. Most of them don't care much—if they see me with her, they know she's off the market. It's ironic because she's technically not off the market, not yet anyway. Maybe by the end of the night, I'll have the guts to ask her out on a real date, one where I drive and pick her up even if she does live across town.

I pull on my confident personality, the one that's been perfected over years of being thrown unwillingly into the popularity spotlight, and it seems to put Jules at ease. She laughs at my jokes and chats with my friends, and beats me at a game of air hockey. I'm not sure if this is a real date, but I like whatever it is. We're having fun. And it sure beats when I'm normally at these parties by myself and I either spend all night hanging out with my teammates, who I see all the time anyway, or being bombarded by girls who flirt with me constantly even though I don't like them.

Hanging out with Jules is a kind of fun I didn't know I could have. She's sweet and seems to like being around me, but she's also not throwing herself at me. I know my guy friends like to rag on me, saying I don't appreciate how "lucky" I am for having girls fawn over me all the time, but I hate that. I just want to be normal. I don't want to be the guy girls like because he's popular. Jules makes me feel like a normal high school guy, not like some pseudo celebrity. It's refreshing.

Jules tugs on my sleeve after we watch Oliver and Chase battle it out for air hockey champion. "Hey?" she says. "Where's the bathroom?"

"It's down that hallway all the way to the end, on the left," I say, pointing toward the hallway. "There's another one in the kitchen but it's usually occupied. No one knows about the hallway one."

"You're the best," she says. She holds out her plastic cup. "Do you mind holding this for me?"

"Not at all." I take her cup and she slips off into the crowd of people. Not two seconds later, Trevor Blankenship appears beside me. I know him by name only, and we've never talked, I don't think. Now he's staring at me like we're best friends or something.

"Hey, man," he says with a nod. "You dating Jules?"

I have no idea why he seems to care so much, but before I can answer, Oliver walks up beside me and says, "Why, you jealous?"

Trevor just snorts. "I was just wondering. We all

want to know when the hottest guy in school will finally be off the market."

"Why?" Oliver says. "It's not like the girls would want to date you anyhow."

"Funny man with funny jokes," Trevor says, rolling his eyes.

I laugh along with them, but I don't say anything and luckily Trevor walks away a few seconds later. Truth is, I wish I could tell them that I'm dating Jules. Hopefully it'll be something I can say soon. Until then, I'm not going to ruin it by implying anything.

Oliver challenges me to a game of air hockey, and I set Jules' cup down on the edge of the air hockey table. After a few minutes go by, I'm wondering where she is and if she got lost on her way to the bathroom. There are two hallways that branch off from Oliver's huge game room—maybe she went to the wrong one.

I'm thinking about her too much and I don't pay enough attention to the game, which gives Oliver the advantage. He scores seven points against me while I only get two on him, and soon the game is over. While Oliver is gloating about his epic win, I glance around, looking for Jules.

When I find her, my heart sinks. All these giddy

feelings of happiness I've had with her all night seem to crash and burn, lighting up a deep pain in my chest.

She didn't get lost, after all. She just started talking to Trevor.

He's got her captivated while they talk in the corner of the room, his hand on the wall next to her shoulder while he leans in closely, telling her what could be any number of romantic things.

I realize now, like a complete fool, that Trevor wasn't asking about my dating life to see if I was off the market.

He was asking to see if she was.

ELEVEN

JULES

I KNOW THERE WASN'T ANY ALCOHOL IN MY drink, but I'm starting to wonder if I'm drunk.

I've never actually been drunk, but I've heard it's a lot like when you're super sick and haven't slept in days and have taken a lot of cold medicine. I feel kind of like that right now, because Trevor is talking to me.

And he's telling me everything I've wanted to hear for so long. All the things I thought I'd never hear—he's saying them.

Surely, I'm drunk.

Maybe there's some kind of toxic mold in the air that's causing hallucinations and I'm not actually talking to Trevor right now, but some kind of house-plant that I only think is Trevor.

Yep. That would make way more sense than what it looks like is happening right now.

"I'm serious, babe," Trevor says. (or, possibly the houseplant says) He reaches up and touches my cheek, which makes me flinch. He hasn't touched me since before he dumped me on social media. "I miss you."

"You broke up with me," I manage to say even though my throat is dry and my heart is pounding and I'm still kind of questioning that whole hallucinating/drunk thing.

"I still miss you," he says, leaning a bit closer. I can smell his cologne and it brings back so many memories, both painful and happy. "Breaking up with you was a mistake."

I look into his eyes and feel an overwhelming urge to turn back time, back to when I was happy and I thought we were in love. I don't even think it's Trevor that does this to me—it's the feelings. The memories of being happy. Feeling worthy. It's not him at all, it's just what I wish I could feel instead of right now because all I feel now is sadness and desperation. I spent all summer and these first couple weeks of school wishing I didn't feel this way. I've sworn off boys, and yet here I am at a party with Jake even though I'm not allowed to like him.

And now Trevor is here?

No. This can't happen. I refuse to let my ex-boyfriend come back into my life and ruin things again. Agreeing to come to this party with Jake was equally stupid. I am not going to date anyone this year, and I'm really not going to get back with my ex. I am too smart for this nonsense.

I have to protect my heart.

I put my hand on Trevor's shoulder and push him away from me. "I have to go," I say, walking straight forward. I ignore my ex as he calls my name. I expect him to follow, and I expect to have to ignore him but he doesn't follow after me.

I guess that's what I should have expected instead. He only cares about me a slight bit. He's not "all in" when it comes to dating me. If I were to have agreed to date him again tonight, then he'd only end up hurting me again.

And that's exactly why I have to leave.

When I get to the front door, I slip outside unnoticed. Everyone here at the party is too busy doing their own thing to notice the quiet girl from school walking out alone. While I want nothing to do with Trevor, and I'll never date someone super popular like Jake, I don't want to make him think I got kidnapped or something, so I take out my phone and text Jake from the quiet darkness of my car.

I'm feeling sick so I'm heading home early.
See you in class on Monday!

I'm not sure if that sounds believable, but at this point I don't care. All that matters is making sure I don't ever let a guy hurt my heart again.

TWELVE

JAKE

I'M PRETENDING TO WATCH MY FRIENDS PLAY A game of pool when I get Jules' text. She couldn't even have the courage to tell me the truth, that she's decided to spend the rest of the night with Trevor instead of me. No, she made up some story about feeling sick. My heart aches for a few seconds, and the pain is unbearable. I try to tell myself to get mad, not sad. To tell myself I'll just find another girl to crush on—Jules isn't that great. The words fall flat in my mind because they aren't true.

I can tell myself I'm mad and not sad, but I don't believe it. I don't want another girl to crush on. I wanted Jules. She's become a good friend in math class and talking with her on Snapchat is the highlight of my day. My little brother asks about her all the time. I want her in my life.

The crushing, brutal truth is that I wanted to date her, and she wanted Trevor over me. I am a total idiot. Trevor isn't the hottest guy in school—I am. I guess this goes to prove that she's even better of a person than I thought because she chose him over me when most girls would choose me just so they're dating the popular guy. Jules isn't like that, though. She doesn't care about high school popularity, and that's one of the reasons I really liked her.

Now she's Trevor's girl.

I head to the kitchen to grab a soda, hoping the sugar and caffeine will somehow drown my broken heart. But the second I see the back of Trevor's letterman jacket, my heart tightens. He's here. But the girl he's got his arm slung around isn't Jules...

I walk past him trying to be casual, but he doesn't seem to notice me. He's too busy trying to get this girl's number. I don't see Jules anywhere. Maybe she did go home. Maybe she is sick.

Maybe I just spent the last twenty minutes thinking she lied to me for nothing. Maybe she didn't lie at all—and that possibility actually sounds a lot more like Jules. Now I feel awful. I crack open my soda can and drink half of it as I walk out to my truck and get inside, drowning out the loud music and laughter from the party in the house. If Jules isn't at the party anymore, I don't want to be here, either. Before I go home, I decide to reach out one more time.

I pull up Snapchat and send her a message.

Are you okay? Need anything?

Snapchat tells you when someone reads your message, and within about thirty seconds, I can see that Jules read it. But she doesn't reply right away. I sit here staring at my phone for five minutes, then ten, and still no reply. I'm about to send a second message—which all my friends tell me is the worst thing you can do because double messaging makes it look like you're too eager—when Jules finally replies.

I'm fine. Just a headache.

Why do I feel like that's not the entire truth?

I send her back a sad face emoji and tell her I

hope she feels better soon. She reads the message and sends back a "thanks". It doesn't feel sincere. I know we aren't best friends or anything but I feel like I know her better than that. Something is wrong with her, and I don't think it's a headache.

I just wish we were close enough for her to tell me the truth.

THIRTEEN

Tears stream down my face as I drive away from Oliver's neighborhood. There's a lump in my throat the size of Texas and no matter how many deep breaths I take, I can't seem to make it go away. I am overwhelmed with the annoying realization that I can't just say something and make it true. I couldn't just tell myself to get over Trevor breaking my heart. I can't just tell myself to not crush on anyone this year. Especially not when the guy in question is Jake Johnson, Hottest Guy in School.

And he's so much more than that, so much more than anyone gives him credit for. He's incredibly smart and he's kind and he doesn't lose his patience with me when it's taking me longer than it should to figure out a math problem. He asks how my weekend went and he remembers the random things I tell him about myself in class. He could easily be the most stuck up guy in school with how popular he is, but he's not. He seems like a good guy on the inside, and outside.

That's why it's so hard not to like him.

Every single thing inside of me, from my heart to my head and even deep down in my toes, wants to like Jake. I want to crush on him so hard and swoon over him and spend all night looking into his dreamy eyes while hanging out at that party I just left. But I can't.

I can't let myself like Jake the way I used to like Trevor. We can see how well that turned out for me. I gave my heart to Trevor and he smashed it open on social media, breaking up with me publicly for everyone to see. And then he had the nerve to talk to me at that party just now, as if I'd ever be stupid enough to take him back! Yeah freaking right. Not happening.

I might have been stupid enough to date him once, but I'm not stupid enough to do it again.

Leaving this party was my only option. I have to make a conscious effort to protect my heart this year or it'll just get broken again.

I wipe away my tears and stare out at the road ahead of me. It's still two hours before my curfew, and I'm trying not to think about what kind of a loser I am for coming home early. Most teenagers beg to stay out later. I breathe out a deep sigh and tell myself to stop thinking about Jake.

There's a loud *pop* and then my car jolts. Crap. My tire is flat.

The steering wheel wobbles as I edge my car over to the side of the road and stop the engine. I've never had a flat tire before, but it's pretty obvious that's the problem before I get out and look because the sound was unmistakably the sound of a tire popping.

Sure enough, my front driver's side tire is flattened like a pancake, and here I am stuck on the side of a back road that hardly anyone ever drives down. I call my dad and the phone rings and rings, but he doesn't answer. It's 9:30 at night and he's probably already asleep. I call my mom's phone too but she keeps it on silent most of the time, so it's no surprise when she doesn't answer. I call Dad again, and still no answer.

I heave a sigh and kick the flat tire in frustration. I could be dying here on the side of the road and my parents wouldn't even know! Ugh!

I don't know who else to call, so I call my best friend. Abby doesn't have a car, but maybe she can borrow Abuela's.

"Abuela is at bingo," Abby says with a frustrated groan. "I'm sorry! She usually doesn't get home until midnight or so. You know how wild those old lady bingo nights can get."

"I'll just have to change the tire myself," I say as I kneel down and stare at the thing on my car.

"Do you know how?" Abby asks.

"No," I admit. "But there's a spare tire in my trunk and all the tools that come with it. Maybe there's instructions or something. Why didn't I ever figure out how to do this particular skill before I needed it?

"Look it up on YouTube," Abby says. "YouTube can teach you anything."

"Good call," I say. "I'll let you know when I figure it out."

"Okay, be safe," she says. "Don't get murdered."

I wasn't thinking about getting murdered until she said it, and now here I am in the dark, on the side of the road, in the middle of nowhere. This is a prime place to get murdered. Anxiety tries to take over as I watch a tutorial video on my phone for changing a flat tire. I'm still trying to figure out how to loosen the bolt that holds the spare tire into my trunk when headlights appear from way down the road behind me. Someone is coming. My heart races.

What if it's a murderer? Should I call Abby back? Should I hide in my backseat and hope they drive right on past me?

I grab my phone and turn off the screen, but it's way too late to hide now. Whoever is driving toward me is approaching too fast. They've seen me, there's no doubt about that. I stand tall, hold back tears, and try to act like this is no big deal. Maybe they'll just drive right on by.

But the vehicle slows. Crap. It's definitely slowing down to stop.

Crap, crap, crap.

I try not to panic as the truck comes to a complete stop several yards behind me. The head-lights are so bright I can't see anything else, but I hear the door open and close, and then the sounds of someone walking toward me. I see the shadow of a body breaking through the bright headlight beams.

This is it. I really hope I'm not about to be murdered.

Then the guy steps closer and I can see his face.

Relief hits me first, but then anxiety comes rushing back ten times harder than before. Maybe a murderer would have been easier to deal with right now, than the guy standing in front of me.

Jake.

FOURTEEN

JAKE

I DIDN'T RECOGNIZE HER CAR AT FIRST. ANYTIME I see someone stranded on the side of the road, I'll stop and see if I can help them, so that's what I was doing. To my surprise, the stranded motorist is Jules, the girl I've been thinking of nonstop since I saw her with Trevor.

"Hey," I say, walking up to her. She's staring at me, quite literally like a deer in the headlights, her eyes squinting.

"Jake?" she says, shielding her eyes from the bright headlights of my truck. "What are you doing here?"

"I was just going home," I say.

"Why so early?"

I shrug. No need to tell her I left because if she

wasn't at the party, I didn't want to be there either. "Are you okay? How's your head?"

"Oh, my tire is flat," she says, looking back at her car. "I didn't get in a wreck or anything so my head is fine."

I lift an eyebrow. The flat tire is obvious—it's the first thing I saw when I walked up. "No, I mean... your head? Your headache? The reason you left the party early?"

"Oh!" she says, eyes widening in recognition. She flattens her palm to the side of her head. "Yeah, it still hurts. Not too bad, though."

That was weird. It kind of makes me think she doesn't have a headache at all. But I don't know why she would lie about something like that. Maybe inviting her to the party was a bad idea. I wish I had just gotten the courage to ask her on a real date, just the two of us somewhere romantic without people like Trevor around.

"Let me help you with your tire," I say. She already has her trunk opened, and I lift up the bottom flooring panel and remove the spare tire.

"I have a YouTube video," she says, holding out her phone. "I found one for my exact type of car so it has step by step instructions."

I smirk. "I know how to change a tire... I don't

need a video."

She looks sheepish as she puts her phone away. "Okay. Well, thanks. I really appreciate this."

"I'm happy to help," I say as I unload her spare tire and set it on the ground. "Oh... that's not good."

I kneel down and look at the spare. It's a standard donut that comes with the car, not a full size replacement tire. And it's just as flat as the tire on her car. This thing has probably never been serviced since the car was purchased over ten years ago.

"What's wrong?" Jules says. She kneels down beside me, bringing the sweet scent of her perfume with her. She looks at the spare tire and then back at me. "It's flat."

"Yep," I say with a nod. I stand back up and put the spare back into her trunk. "There's no way this tire would work. It's too flat. Looks dry-rotted."

She sighs. "So what do I do? Call some kind of tow truck or something?"

"Getting a tow is expensive this late at night. I'd wait until the morning and then it'll be a lot cheaper. But that's only if you want to leave your car here overnight. I'd be happy to drive you home."

Her lips slide to the side of her mouth as she considers it. "Well, if I take my purse with me, then there's nothing valuable in here. Do you think it would get vandalized?"

I look up and down this long country road in the middle of nowhere. "I really doubt it. This is a pretty good town and people take care of each other here."

"True," she says. "That's why my parents love living in a small town. Okay, I guess I'll just leave it. I tried calling my parents but they're asleep. I don't know what else they'd expect me to do in a situation like this."

"At least I'm here and not some creepy stranger," I say with a smile.

She smiles back. Every time she smiles back at me, I can't help but feel those butterflies in my stomach. It makes me all stupid inside.

In a good way. A very good way.

"Thanks," she says after she grabs her purse from inside her car. She locks the doors and then slides the purse over her shoulder. "I guess we can go now."

I have the urge to open the passenger door for her, but then I realize that giving a girl a ride home when she's stranded on the side of the road is definitely not a date, and not a time for me to be some kind of hopeless romantic. I let her get her own door and I climb into the driver's seat. "Where to?" I ask as I drive away in the direction her car was going before she got a flat tire.

"Head toward the high school," she says while she stares at her phone. The screen lights up her beautiful features and she's so gorgeous it's hard to keep my eyes on the road.

The high school is only a couple miles away, and it's also in the direction of my house. We ride in a comfortable silence for a few minutes, the radio playing softly in the background. It's not until she points up ahead and says, "Turn right at Glenrock," that things get weird.

"Glenrock?" I say, just to make sure I heard her correctly.

She nods. I turn down the street, which is the entrance to my own subdivision. She points to the left. "Take the second left."

I turn, and she directs me to her driveway. I park and look over at her. "You know this is two streets away from my house, right?"

Of course she knows... she's been to my house. But that's not why I'm asking. I'm asking because just earlier today she told me it wouldn't make sense for me to pick her up and drive her to the party. She said we lived too far away from each other. But clearly, that was a lie.

And now she knows that *I know* she lied.

She bites her lip. "I'm... sorry."

"Why didn't you want me to drive us to the party?" I ask.

She looks at me for a long moment, and each second that passes makes me feel worse, not better. Then she takes a ragged breath. "I don't know," she says, reaching for the door handle. "But I have to go."

And then just like that, she leaves. I watch her walk up to her front door and slip inside her house, leaving me here in a driveway that's just a few seconds away from my own, wondering why the girl of my dreams lied and told me she lived far away.

FIFTEEN

The moment I get to my bedroom I burst into tears. How could I have been so unbelievably stupid? I lied and left the party early just to get away from boys and then Fate swooped in and said, "No Jules... you don't get to sneak out of this party on a lie. I'm going to reveal your lies to everyone because I hate you."

Thanks a lot, Fate. You're the worst.

How could I have been so stupid? Ugh. I drop onto my bed without bothering to shower or brush my teeth because I'm so disgusted and sad and humiliated that none of those basic hygienic things matter to me right now. I can't believe I told Jake where I lived when I knew I had lied to him about it. I guess I thought I could have kept up this lie forever, because I was never supposed to crush on Jake and I definitely never should have hung out with him. If I had done what I was supposed to do and kept him at arm's length, kept him as a random guy at school that I didn't care about, then he'd never have discovered where I lived.

If I was smart, I'd have given him directions to Abby's house and just pretended I lived there. If I was smart, I wouldn't have gone to the party at all, and then I wouldn't have seen Trevor, either.

Being smart would have saved me a lot of heartache.

I'm on my bed staring at the ceiling for another hour when the tears finally start to fade away. Now I'm just humiliated but no longer crying, so I guess that's an improvement. After wiping away my tears, I go take a hot shower and think about what I'm going to do with myself. There's no way I can go back to math class on Monday. I straight up lied to Jake and told him I lived far away when I knew I lived within walking distance. How do you come back from that?

A little voice in my head tells me that this is exactly why I swore off boys this year. They're just too complicated. You can't like them because they'll hurt you. You can't avoid them because you'll end up embarrassing yourself. I am just totally screwed no matter what I do. I can't believe I thought for just one second that I could get through this year of school without any boy drama.

I don't know how I fall asleep, but eventually I do. When I wake up in the morning, my dad is calling my name in a frenzy. He'd woken up and went outside to get the newspaper only to see that my car wasn't in the driveway. Then he panicked and thought I hadn't come home. He and my mom give me this huge lecture about how it's incredibly important to tell them if something like that happens... and then I told them to check their cell phones. They saw my many messages and missed calls and then apologized.

All the parental drama keeps me occupied for about ten minutes, and then I'm once again back to being humiliated about what happened with Jake last night. Dad takes me to the tire shop to buy a new tire and then we drive out to where my car was left overnight. Luckily, no one messed with it, just like Jake and I had assumed. I help my dad change the tire out and then I drive home feeling nervous and awkward and ten kinds of mad at myself for getting into this mess. How am I supposed to face Jake again?

I told him a pretty big lie about living far away. I

used to think I was at least semi-smart, but now I can't think of any possible explanation that would explain why I told that lie, at least not an explanation that doesn't embarrass me. I could claim temporary amnesia. Or temporary insanity. But it's not like he'd believe any of that. Jake knows me pretty well after spending a few weeks of class with me. Crap.

By Sunday night, the only plan I have is a pretty stupid one. I fake sick.

Mom believes it and lets me stay home on Monday. Then again on Tuesday.

But by Wednesday, I think she's onto me. She sits on my bed in the morning, the back of her hand pressed against my forehead. She frowns. "You don't have a fever. And your skin isn't flushed. You look fine."

"I feel terrible," I say, snuggling deeper into my blankets.

"Oh yeah?" Mom crosses her hands over her chest. "What are your symptoms?"

Uh oh. I should have thought of that before faking sick. She didn't question me the last two days but now she's giving me that classic Mom Look and I know I've tested her trust a little too far. Outside, a crack of lightning zaps through the sky and the morning sunlight is shadowed by dark storm clouds.

"My throat hurts," I say, adding in a wince for good measure. "And my head hurts. Everything just hurts. Maybe it's the flu."

Mom laughs. "Nice try. Go to school."

"Mom!" I whine as another loud boom of thunder fills the air. "It's about to rain outside!"

"So I suggest you bring an umbrella." Mom shakes her head. "I know a faker when I see one. Go to school or you're grounded. Rain or not."

With that declaration of awfulness, she leaves. I climb out of bed and get dressed, moving slowly and with all the eagerness of a sloth. My stomach hurts. Mr. Casey's class is the first class of the day and I have no idea how I'm going to face Jake. I haven't even read the last two Snapchat messages he sent me yesterday, but I'm guessing they have something to do with asking why I wasn't at school. I can't face him. Not after what happened between us. I still don't have a good excuse.

The sky is almost pitch black from storm clouds, and it keeps lighting up with streaks of lightning and the boom of an occasional thunder, but luckily, it's not raining yet. As I walk into the high school, I realize that maybe I don't need an excuse. Maybe I can just run away. Not literally, of course... but figuratively. I could be somewhere else instead of Mr. Casey's first period math class. Then I could just go the rest of my high school life carefully trying to avoid Jake Johnson forever. Should be easy, right?

Instead of meeting Abby and getting a coffee, I walk to the counselor's office. Mrs. Baker is sitting at her desk sipping her own coffee when I walk in.

"I need a schedule change," I say.

She sets her coffee cup down. "Good morning to you, too, Miss Minuti. Why do you need a schedule change?"

"I feel that—my schedule would be better if—" A sudden alarm goes off, interrupting my stuttering reply while I tried to think of an excuse to change my schedule. It sounds a lot like a fire alarm, only slightly different. Mrs. Baker stands up, eyebrows pulled together.

An announcement comes over the speaker a minute later. "Please disregard."

"That's weird," Mrs. Baker says. "I know the weather is bad but..." She glances out the window in her office, where the rain has finally unleashed itself onto the parking lot. Then she looks at me. "Wait here."

She steps outside of her office and stops short, looking at someone who is just to her right, but hidden from my view by the door. "Why are you here?" she says.

"I want to change my schedule."

Chills prickle over my skin when I hear Jake's voice. I haven't seen him in a few days but I'd recognize his voice anywhere.

"Wait in my office," she says as she walks away.

I brace myself as Jake enters. His eyes widen as he steps into the small office and sees me sitting here in one of the two chairs across from Mrs. Baker's desk. He stops short, his hand reaching up to scratch the back of his neck. "Hi," he says.

"Schedule change?" I say.

He nods. "You?"

"Same."

He sits in the chair next to me and looks out the large square window behind Mrs. Baker's desk. "Are you trying to get away from me in first period?"

"Are you trying to get away from me in first period?" I say in rebuttal.

Jake looks over at me. His eyes are filled with a sadness I didn't expect. He looks truly hurt, and now I feel even worse for lying to him, avoiding him, and then trying to get my schedule changed.

"Jake... I—"

The lights go off.

SIXTEEN

JAKE

Everything goes dark. And silent. The lights didn't just go out—all of the power did, and now the hum of the air conditioning and the soft sound of Mrs. Baker's computer running have all been silenced, leaving only Jules and me sitting here, alone, quiet, and bathed in the darkness of the cloudy stormy sky outside the window.

"I'm sorry for whatever I did," I say over the lump in my throat. "I never meant for things to be weird between us."

"No, it's my fault." Jules exhales. "I'm sorry I lied to you about where I lived," she says, her voice the only sound in the room. She's all shadowy across from me, but I think she's looking my way. "I shouldn't have lied to you and I'm sorry."

"Can I ask why you lied?"

She's quiet for a minute. "It's not because of you... like... it's nothing you did. I'm just—I just..." She sighs again. "It's just all me. I did it for reasons I can't tell you and trust me, if you knew, you'd laugh."

Another loud alarm pierces the air, making us both jump. Mrs. Baker rushes back into her office looking flustered. "Good, you're both here," she says. "The halls are a madhouse since class hasn't started yet. They're putting everyone in lockdown so I need you two to stay here."

Jules and I exchange worried looks. An announcement crackles over the speaker in the ceiling: "Attention Brazos High School. We are under a tornado warning. Tornadoes have been spotted in the area, and we need to shelter in place. Please go into the nearest classroom immediately."

The lights flicker on and then back off again. There's a soft glow from one of the emergency lights in the hallway, which illuminates Mrs. Baker's blonde hair. "You two stay here."

"Isn't that window kind of a safety hazard?" I ask.

Mrs. Baker stares at it and then shrugs. "Maybe. Get on the floor, use my desk as a shield. You'll be fine. I'll be back in a few minutes."

And then she closes her office door, leaving me here with the girl I'm crushing hard on, alone in a dark office.

Jules and I drop to the floor, our backs pressed up against Mrs. Baker's large wooden desk, which separates us from the window on the opposite wall. I can barely see her to my right because the room is too dark. Every few seconds, a bolt of lightning will flash across the sky, lighting up the room for a split second.

"Well this is romantic," I say sarcastically.

Jules doesn't say anything, which makes my stupid joke feel ten times stupider.

"I guess we both don't have to leave Mr. Casey's class," I say, trying to make some kind of conversation because sitting here in a dark room with Jules while the weather alarm goes off is the most awkward thing ever. "I'll see if I can change classes and you can stay that way your schedule doesn't get messed up."

"I'll change classes," she says. "I'm the reason we're in this mess, so there's no need for you to mess up your schedule."

"I don't mind," I say. A flash of lightning bursts through the room and I can see her face for just a moment, looking right at me. "Or... we could just stay partners?"

"Wouldn't that be weird?"

I shrug. "Not if we don't make it weird. I mean... we're friends, right?"

She exhales. "You are really, really nice, Jake. I'm sorry I lied to you. I really am. You're cool. We should be friends."

"Yeah?" I say, feeling relieved that she doesn't hate me.

"Yeah," she says softly. "Friends."

Then my heart cracks open just a bit. Friends. That's not what I want to be with Jules. I want to be so much more than that. The rain pelts against the window, loudly drowning out my thoughts. Thunder rolls through the sky, and the entire building sounds like it's being attacked by a mega-villain rainstorm. Jules and I sit quietly for a long while, just listening to the rain. And then something happens in me. A shift, a change in my entire heart. I don't know why, but suddenly I feel like I can't keep this to myself. I can't just sit here, content with being *friends*.

"Jules... I like you," I say. My voice fills the small room, my words drifting across all of this silence that had been settled between us. And once I've started talking, I realize I can't stop. "I really like you. I like you as more than a friend."

I glance over at her, but the sky stays dark, no lightning to show me a hint of what she might be thinking right now. Doesn't matter. I've started talking and now I'm going to say everything I want to say. If she hates me when it's over, then oh well. At least I would have been able to say what's on my heart.

"Jules... the thing is... I've never had a girlfriend."

I hear her gasp in the darkness, and it makes me snort out a sarcastic laugh. "Yeah. I'm not lying. It's the truth. Everyone thinks I'm so popular and... well, you know. They just assume I date a lot and the truth is that I never have."

"Why are you telling me this?" Jules says.

"I don't know. I just wanted you to know the truth." I run a hand through my hair. "I really like you, and I should have asked you on a real date and not to Oliver's stupid party. I just have no idea what I'm doing when it comes to dating."

"In the name of embarrassing confessions..." Jules says softly. "I guess I can tell you something, too."

My heart skips a beat. "Please do. Make it extra embarrassing, please. I'm mortified over here."

She laughs. "Well, how's this for embarrassing...

my boyfriend dumped me last year and broke my heart and made me so sad that I promised myself I wouldn't date anyone this year. And then I somehow get seated next to the hottest guy in school, and Mr. Casey forces us to be friends and well..." She heaves a sigh. "Somehow, I stupidly got a crush on you."

"And that's bad...?"

"Yeah, it's bad!" In the shadows I think I see her throw her arms in the air. "I can't have a crush on any guy this year, and I really can't have a crush on you."

"Why?" I ask. "What's so wrong with me?"

"You're the *hottest guy in school*." She says it like she's saying my yearbook superlative title and not like she's just calling me hot. "I can't crush on you. You're way out of my league."

"Jules, you are so in my league."

She goes quiet for a minute. "I don't know what to say."

"Why can't you crush on me?" I ask. "I mean... if it wasn't for my stupid looks?"

"I can't crush on anyone," she says. "I refuse to get hurt again."

"What if I won't hurt you?"

Lightning strikes outside, and it's one of those long ones that light up the sky for about five seconds.

Jules looks over at me and our eyes meet, sending a bolt of another type of electricity right through my body.

"Jake…" she says softly. "I don't want to get hurt again. I don't want to crush on the most popular guy in school. I don't want to feel as bad as I felt when Trevor broke up with me last year. I just can't deal with that kind of pain again."

I reach over and take her hand in the shadows. "What if we just trust each other?"

"Jake…"

"I'm serious," I say, squeezing her hand. "I really like you. I like everything about you. I know it's probably a weird thing to date me with my stupid popularity but I'll do whatever it takes to make it easier on you, I promise. I really, really wish you'd give me a chance. I promise I won't hurt you."

"And what if I hurt you?" she says.

I trace my thumb across her palm. "That's a risk I'm willing to take just to know what it's like to be your boyfriend."

I hear her gulp. "Are you asking me out?"

"Yes," I say. "Sorry I'm doing such a bad job of it."

She sits up on her knees and scoots closer to me.

"You're not doing a bad job. I kind of like this whole honesty thing."

The lights come back on and suddenly I'm staring into the eyes of the most beautiful girl. And I'm still holding her hand. She reaches out and takes my other hand. And then I kiss her.

EPILOGUE

Jake

Two weeks later

I squeeze Jules' hand as we walk through the hallways of Brazos High School, making our way toward Mr. Casey's first period math class. All around us, girls are watching her, and me, and us. It's like the entire school can't get over seeing me with an actual girlfriend after years of only hearing about my supposed female conquests. With the way some people watch us, you'd think their heads might explode off their shoulders any minute now.

"I'm sorry about the stares," I whisper.

Jules shrugs and smiles up at me. "I'm used to it

by now."

"You are the greatest girlfriend on the planet."

Jules rolls her eyes and takes a sip of her coffee. "Until you've dated every girl on the planet, you can't exactly make that statement. You have no idea if it's true."

"I don't want to date every girl on the planet." I lean over and kiss the top of her head. Now that Jules is officially my girlfriend, I get to do all the cute things I've always wanted to do—like kissing her head. "I just want to date you."

She makes that little grin that always sends my heart racing. It's a look she only gives to me, and it's part bashful, part flirty. It's one of my favorite things about her.

"Oh my gosh," Abby says sarcastically. "Would you two stop doing that *looking longingly into each other's eyes* thing? It's so annoying to those of us who are single."

I know she's mostly playing with us, but I've also been in Abby's shoes before, watching all the happy couples around you and wishing you were also part of a happy couple. I feel bad now.

"Sorry," I say.

"It's fine," Abby says with a sigh. "I'm happy that you make Jules happy."

"You just need to start dating one of Jake's hot soccer friends," Jules says, wiggling her eyebrows at her best friend. "Then we can all go on double dates."

Abby's tanned cheeks turn pink. "Yeah, right. A hot soccer guy won't like me."

"Yes they will! I bet all of his friends would like you." Jules turns to me. "Right?"

"Well... I'm not sure you'd want to date some of the guys on the team..." I curl my lip, thinking of that party the guys threw before school started. "Some of them are total players I wouldn't trust around any girl. But some of them are good guys, too."

Abby sips her coffee and then stops when we reach Mr. Casey's classroom. This is where she leaves us each morning. "We are so not talking about my dating life right now. That is way too embarrassing."

"Fine, we'll talk about it later," Jules says.

Abby rolls her eyes and then walks away. In class, I slide into my desk right next to my desk partner, who is now my first girlfriend ever and also favorite person on earth. When the class begins, Mr. Casey walks right in front of my desk, a big grin on his face.

"Everyone," he says, projecting his voice across

the classroom. "I am proud of what everyone has accomplished so far this year, but I'd like to take a second to point out that this partnership right here —" He holds out both hands toward Jules and me— "has scored the first ever one hundred percent on an exam in my class. Congratulations, you two."

Some of our classmates make sarcastic comments, and a couple of them clap for us. Most people don't really care, despite how much Mr. Casey tries to make everyone care about his class, but that's just the nature of being in high school, I guess. Luckily, he doesn't make us the spotlight for too long, because after that announcement, he turns around and walks back up to the whiteboard to begin his new lesson.

"Wow," Jules says to me. "We're amazing."

"Yes we are," I say, winking at her. "We're the best."

Want to get an email when Amy's next book is released? Sign up for her newsletter here and get exclusive access to giveaways, new releases, and more!

Sign up here: http://eepurl.com/bTmkPX

ABOUT THE AUTHOR

Amy Sparling is the bestselling author of books for teens and the teens at heart. She lives on the coast of Texas with her family, her spoiled rotten pets, and a huge pile of books. She graduated with a degree in English and has worked at a bookstore, coffee shop, and a fashion boutique. Her fashion skills aren't the best, but luckily she turned her love of coffee and books into a writing career that means she can work in her pajamas. Her favorite things are coffee, book boyfriends, and Netflix binges.

She's always loved reading books from R. L. Stine's Fear Street series, to The Baby Sitter's Club series by Ann, Martin, and of course, Twilight. She started writing her own books in 2010 and now publishes several books a year. Amy loves getting messages from her readers and responds to every single one! Connect with her on one of the links below.